This Little Tiger book belongs to:

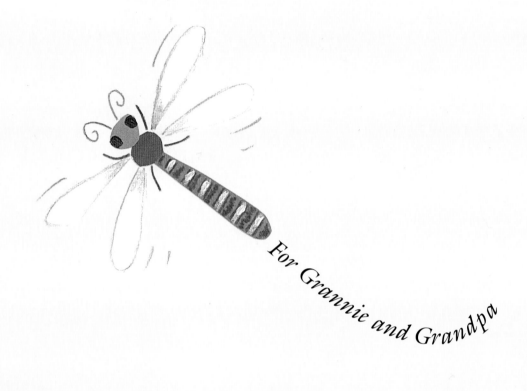

For Grannie and Grandpa

This edition produced 2005 for
BOOKS ARE FUN LTD
1680 Hwy 1 North, Fairfield, Iowa, IA 52556

by LITTLE TIGER PRESS
An imprint of Magi Publications
1 The Coda Centre, 189 Munster Road, London SW6 6AW
www.littletigerpress.com

Originally published in Great Britain 2000 by Little Tiger Press, London

Text and illustrations copyright © Joanne Partis 2000

Printed in China

2 4 6 8 10 9 7 5 3 1

Joanne Partis

Hungry Harry

LITTLE TIGER PRESS

Harry Frog was feeling hungry.
"What's for dinner?" he asked his mom.
"Well, I think you're old enough to look for
your own food now," said Mommy Frog.

"Terrific!" cried Harry, and off
he leaped across the lily pond . . .

till he came to some tall reeds.
"There's sure to be something tasty
here," said Harry, licking his lips.

Sure enough, there was a delicious-looking dragonfly. Harry was just about to jump when . . .

the dragonfly flew off, high
into the air.
"You can't eat me!" she called.
"I'm much too quick for you."

Harry was wondering
what to do next when
suddenly he saw . . .

a big juicy caterpillar
on a twig above him.

"Goody, goody, dinner at last!" cried Harry, but when he flicked out his long tongue to catch it . . .

the caterpillar laughed. "You can't eat me!" she said. "My hairs would tickle your tongue."

"Never mind, I'll find something soon," said Harry.
He bounced on until he met . . .

a scrumptious-looking snail crawling towards him.

"Yummy, yummy," said Harry, but when he reached it . . .

the snail's head suddenly disappeared!
"You can't eat me!" said the
snail from inside its shell.
"I'm much too clever."

Harry was getting hungrier and hungrier.
He was just about to give up and go
home to his mom, when he spotted . . .

a squirmy worm, wriggling along.
"Now's my chance!" cried Harry, but just as he was about to catch the worm in his big wide mouth . . .

it slithered down into
a wormhole.
"You can't eat me!"
shouted the worm. "I'm
too squiggly and squirmy."

Harry felt
very fed up. He
would go home to
his mom. But just
as he turned to
hop back, he saw
something he'd
never seen
before . . .

It didn't look too quick . . .

It didn't look too tickly . . .

It didn't look too clever . . .

And it didn't look
too squiggly and
squirmy.

In fact it looked . . .

And, what was more . . .

there was eno

ugh for everyone!

Little Tiger Press—books to whet your appetite

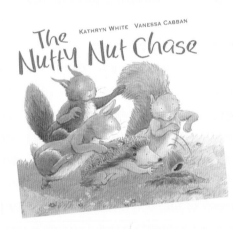

For information regarding any of the above titles, please visit our website:

www.littletigerpress.com